Other Novels by Patricia Perry

The Darkness Trilogy:
Quest for the Source of Darkness
The Fortress of Darkness
The Edge of Darkness: The Final Battle

Short Story

Duchess' Package
Loose Ends: A Hodgepodge of Short Stories
by Authors Without Borders

www.QuestForTheSourceOfDarkness.com

Reviews

The Dean Brothers are wanted neither in Heaven nor Hell. For Lucifer to be successful in keeping the siblings out of the Underworld, he must steer them away from trouble. While Archangels keep watch, the Devil lurches from one crisis to another as he finds the task increasingly difficult to complete. *Old Gooseberry's Dilemma* is a devilishly entertaining story with a sting in its tale, or should that be tail?

Brian R Hill,
Author of ***The Shintae***

Old Gooseberry's Dilemma is an unexpectedly funny and delightful novella offering a fresh and unique perspective of how each of us is watched-over from above. The interaction of supernatural characters that take on human traits, made me chuckle-out-loud. Heaven and Hell will never be thought of in the same old way again. An unpredictable ending was the frosting on this cake!

Thomas Cirignano, Author of
The Constant Outsider: Memoirs of a South Boston Mechanic, www.TheConstantOutsider.com

I was absolutely fascinated by the imagination of author Patricia Perry to think of writing *Old Gooseberry's Dilemma* about the devil and God. It not only entertained me all the way through, it made me think about my own life. For a short story, it gives you a reason to wonder how we act with other people in real life situations and the choices we make. Every page pulls you into the next one. Great description!

Author Alberta H. Sequeira
Memoirs: ***A Healing Heart; Someone Stop This Merry-Go-Round; Please God, Not Two***

This book is dedicated to my awesome friends…
you know who you are!

Old Gooseberry's Dilemma

By Patricia Perry

INFINITY
PUBLISHING

All rights reserved. No part of this book shall be reproduced or transmitted in any form or by any means, electronic, mechanical, magnetic, photographic including photocopying, recording or by any information storage and retrieval system, without prior written permission of the publisher. No patent liability is assumed with respect to the use of the information contained herein. Although every precaution has been taken in the preparation of this book, the publisher and author assume no responsibility for errors or omissions. Neither is any liability assumed for damages resulting from the use of the information contained herein.

Copyright © 2010 by Patricia Perry

ISBN 0-7414-6150-1

Printed in the United States of America

This is a work of fiction. Names, characters, places, and incidents either are the product of the author's imagination or are used fictitiously. Any resemblance to actual events or locales or persons, living or dead, is entirely coincidental.

Published October 2010

INFINITY PUBLISHING
1094 New DeHaven Street, Suite 100
West Conshohocken, PA 19428-2713
Toll-free (877) BUY BOOK
Local Phone (610) 941-9999
Fax (610) 941-9959
Info@buybooksontheweb.com
www.buybooksontheweb.com

Table of Contents

Page 1 .... The Meeting

Page 17 .... Wednesday—Late Afternoon

Page 35 .... Thursday Morning

Page 49 .... Thursday—6 p.m.

Page 61 .... Friday—Lunchtime

Page 65 .... Friday—Midnight

Page 75 .... Saturday—6 hours to go

Page 85 .... Saturday—5:55 p.m.

Page 91 .... Saturday—6:00.01 p.m.

The Meeting

God and Lucifer began to have a number of serious discussions concerning Harry and Rex Dean, when the Devil no longer thought the brothers were special and asked God to put them on *his* list. You could well imagine Old Gooseberry stroking his cleanly shaven chin while smirking at some of the brothers' mean but not evil antics. Lucifer thought he had a couple of good prospects and kept an eye out for them, waiting for the brothers to cross over the line but they didn't…well, not really anyway. You see the brothers got involved in some shady stuff but they wouldn't participate in any serious crimes. Harry was impishly irresistible, street smart but had little in the way of book learning under his belt. Deep down inside he wanted to get an education but was too lazy or preoccupied to bother. Rex, on the other hand, was as smooth as a bottle of aged whiskey and always looked out for anything that was free for the taking.

God felt sorry for them and wanted to keep them out of the salivating jaws of Hell. The more chances He gave the brothers, however, the more charmed they felt as they crept closer to the precipice. Lucifer would rub his hands together with delight as the little bits of rock and dirt, dislodged by the brothers' toes, began to fall into that great chasm. The accidents, run-ins with the law and a host of other bad turn of events somehow morphed into good luck for the brothers. Harry and Rex rode the tide of good fortune like surfers catching those perfect waves.

Anyway, back to the meeting between God and Lucifer. It took place in a dilapidated warehouse along the New Bedford waterfront where birds flew unobstructed through broken windows. Gangly weeds poked up through a parking lot composed of little islands of asphalt floating on a sea of gray sand. A rusting chain link fence surrounded most of the abandoned property, which was littered with old tires, heaps of corroding scrap and other junk. Most of the debris had long ago lost its identity and had reverted to indistinguishable blobs. Derelict trucks, their company logos faded by the elements, slouched on deteriorated tires, their broken headlights pointing at the vacant buildings in front of them. The only creatures peering back at the crumbling hulks were rats, cockroaches and pigeons, none of which could insert a key and send some life through their long unused engines. A place once flourishing with the activity encompassing the unloading of fishing boats was now a haven for vermin.

God brought Michael with him, the Archangel picking up the hem of his frock to keep it from getting dirty as they walked over to the building. Lucifer tap-danced around the broken bits of glass, barrels of old oil and dead animals.

They entered the structure from opposite ends, meeting in the middle of the storehouse like a pair of gunslingers waiting for a scheduled shoot-out. Pigeons flew overhead dropping poop upon the dried out wooden planks while rodents scurried into the dark corners. God and Lucifer stopped several paces away from each other, the latter folding his skinny arms across his chest while the former calmly waited for the Devil to speak. The Archangel Michael, his sun streaked shoulder length hair framing his tanned and chiseled face, crossed his brawny arms over his torso. The rivals studied each other for several long moments before Lucifer broke the silence.

"Whatever possessed you to create pigeons?" Lucifer

dodged a dropping. "The vermin I can understand...but those things?"

"I had better plans for them but was distracted just prior to imparting any intelligence into them."

"You should have made up your mind: dirty or stupid—not both," muttered the Devil as an errant feather fell into the mini inferno upon his head. It immediately turned to ash.

"What do you want, Lucifer?" asked the Lord adjusting his white robes. Michael shifted his weight to his right leg then cocked his head and raised a brow at Satan.

"You can have the Deans." *Cheeky bastard*, thought the Devil as he scowled at the angel.

"Why would I want them?"

"I'm going to be very busy in the not too distant future with some unexpected arrivals, leaving me very little time to deal with them."

"I saw the list, Lucifer."

The Devil took a deep breath, the piercing glint in the Lord's eyes freezing him for a split second. Lucifer had greedily helped himself to generous portions of the Deans before finding out they gave him indigestion. He wanted to slip this plate of half-eaten food back onto the banquet table without anyone being the wiser. Satan narrowed his eyes as the Lord waited for him to reply.

Lucifer cleared his throat. "If you saw the files then you know I will be unable to accommodate them."

"My roster is also full," replied the Lord.

"I'll give you ten souls of your choosing."

"Sorry."

"One hundred?"

"I don't think so."

"Paper; rocks and scissors?"

"No."

"I have a quarter."

"No."

"It really does have a head *and* a tail on it…"

"I think not."

"C'mon, G!"

Old Gooseberry closed his eyes and sighed. He squatted on his hindquarters, his wiry frame still except for his forked tail, which flicked back and forth like that of an annoyed cat. Harry and Rex had been so promising. Like every human, they had knapsacks full of sins but not the big ones…ones that would firmly plant them in Hell. As of right now, they were up for grabs with a slight edge to head south: Lucifer needed a trump card but all he had left were jokers.

"Why are you willing to give me the Deans?" inquired God.

Satan used charm, promises and lies to ensnare the unwilling: the Deans, whether they realized it or not, utilized those same methods. Street smarts outfoxed book smarts, for Harry, anyway. That and a healthy dose of providence allowed the brothers to move comfortably on in life despite the occasional hiccup they encountered along the way.

Harry had stolen a few things over his life and beaten up on more than one fool who thought himself more macho. Rex had a unique ability to make people like him, even without resorting to beating the crap out of them.

Lucifer had heard the whispers in Hell, undertones that some of his tormented souls would welcome the Deans to break the monotony of their eternal suffering. The Prince of Darkness, even with all of his powers, would meet his match if Harry and Rex went to Hell. Satan owned the souls of a multitude of wicked people but none with the easy charisma of the brothers. Old Gooseberry glanced over at Michael, his vertical pupils no wider than a strand of hair. The Angels' buff form seemed to dwarf even the massive wings hanging casually from his back as he stared with open amusement at the gaunt devil with the puny leathery wings.

Mine are bigger.

Up yours.

You wish.

Two rats began to fight in a dark corner; their squeals of pain elicited a contented smile on Satan's face. Michael frowned with disgust at the unseen confrontation. It was the one bright moment so far during the meeting and gave Lucifer an idea. Contrary to everything he stood for, Old Gooseberry decided that if he could somehow keep Harry out of trouble then God would be obligated to accept him into Heaven. As nauseating as dabbling in good was at least he wouldn't have to contend with the Dean brothers in *his* house. He mulled over this daunting assignment for a few more moments then glanced over at the waiting pair. Lucifer rose to his feet, shrugged his shoulders in mock defeat then walked out of the warehouse.

God and Michael watched him leave.

"What do you think he is up to, Boss?"

"I don't know but you had better keep a sharp watch over Harry and Rex."

~

Lucifer descended the wide staircase until he reached the bottom, ignoring the lake of molten lava situated in the center of the vast chamber. Tunnels fanned out in every direction, each one holding damned souls according to the degree of their sins. He kept the truly wicked in this room so he could watch them from behind the one-way glass fronting his office. He slapped the back of Adolph's head as the former dictator sat bound and gagged, forced to listen to a Rabbi reading from the Torah. Old Gooseberry had borrowed the Rabbi from Heaven, for in this case both God and the Jewish holy man were more than willing to accommodate the Prince of Darkness. Everybody except for Adolph made out on this compromise. He walked past Jeffrey who sat at a table filled only with fruits and vegetables and disregarded Vlad who tried to thrust a collapsible lance into Idi. He passed through the sulphurous vapors and unbearable heat up to his office and closed the door behind him. The air conditioner hummed softly in the background, muting the screams of the damned. He poured himself a glass of Scotch before plopping down into his sumptuous black leather chair. The Devil propped his feet up on his carved mahogany desk, watching the activity outside his room. Old Gooseberry sighed. All of this could change if Harry and Rex entered his fiery realm. He lit a cigar then grabbed the remote for one of the many television screens, focusing in on Harry while puffing circles of smoke up toward the ceiling.

Harry was at a local bar, the barmaid emphatically pointing first at Harry then the door. He ran his fingers through his dirty blond hair, his red-rimmed blue eyes focused on the thin woman with frizzy brown hair. He waved her off with one hand and banged an empty glass down on the bar with the other, finally storming out of the tavern when she picked up the phone.

Lucifer turned up the volume. A searing string of expletives floated over Harry's shoulder as he stumbled over to his blue pick-up truck. He fumbled with his keys, dropping them several times until he found the lock and opened the door. Harry slid in behind the wheel, stared at the steering column then stuck the key into one of the blurry ignitions wavering before his eyes.

"I hate that bitch…shut me off…." he garbled incessantly. He threw the shifter into reverse, nearly hitting the telephone pole behind him then peeled out down the dimly lit road.

Lucifer dragged his butt to the edge of his chair watching Harry swerving all over the road, fearful he would end up in the morgue before he drove too much farther. This was unacceptable. The Prince of Darkness snapped his fingers, disappearing then reappearing in a cloud of red moments after Harry had sideswiped three cars and mistakenly taken a shortcut down a low alleyway. The truck came to an immediate halt as the roof of the cab became wedged in the passageway. Except for a few slivers of brick and a small shower of mortar, the entranceway held its ground.

"Oh shit!" Taking on a human form, Satan hurried over to

the wreck. He leaned into the vehicle to see how Harry fared. Other than a long and nasty cut, along his forearm, Harry was fine.

"Hey buddy...are you all right?"

"Goddamn it! Who the hell are you...what happened?"

The sound of sirens cut through the night air.

"C'mon...before the cops show up!" Satan pulled Harry from the truck. Too dazed and drunk to argue, Harry allowed the stranger to help him.

Lucifer dragged Harry into the gloomy recesses of the old brick factory where they peeked out at the police converging around the wreckage. The Devil watched the cops surrounded the truck, their flashlights probing the crushed vehicle for signs of life. Or death. Harry collapsed against the Prince of Darkness, belching up cheap whiskey and fried food. Old Gooseberry scowled then grabbed a handful of the mortals' hair, twisting Harry's head until he faced away from him.

"Wasn't that little punk just around here?" asked one of the State Troopers.

"I wonder if he swiped this truck to get away?"

"Over here!" One of the other officers pointed his flashlight at someone running in between the buildings about thirty yards to the right. Most of the police sprinted across the street to pursue him prompting Satan to steer his sagging charge toward freedom. Harry left a trail of glass that fell off his clothing and hair.

"My arm hurts like a bastard."

Lucifer glanced down at the blood collecting on Harry's ripped shirt. He had to get help for the drunk and set the stage to keep the cops from confronting Harry.

"Listen, buddy, the cops were chasing this guy near where you got into that accident. If you play your cards right then you could blame him. Are you listening to me?"

"Who the hell are you?"

"I'm just trying to help you. Now," he pulled Harry into the doorway of a bar and whispered in an almost enticing tone, "tell them you pulled in front of this place and jumped out for only a couple of seconds. Someone stole your truck. *Don't* tell them where it is, got it? Don't forget to call someone to take you to the hospital."

"Why? I'm not sick," his suspicions wafted straight into Lucifer's face, the whiskey vapors so thick they made his eyes water.

"No, but that three inch gash on your arm could use a stitch or two."

Harry looked down at the blood staining his shirt. "Oh shit."

"Yes, well, do what I just told you and here, chew on these." The Devil handed Harry a handful of mints.

"Hey! What's your name?"

Lucifer ignored him. He flagged down a passing patrol car, motioned toward Harry then disappeared around a corner before the cop could ask him any questions. The officer pulled in front of Harry, scrutinizing every square inch of him by the light of his flashlight.

"Hey! You see a guy running by here?"

Harry lifted his arm up. "Get that outta my face!"

"You been drinking?"

Blue flashing lights. A cop asking questions. My arm feels like it's on fire. How did I get in front of this bar?

"Hey—I'm talking to you!"

What did that asshole tell me? Some guy stole and crashed my truck? Oh, shit! He's getting out of his car! Gotta...pull... shit! Gotta think straight!

"How many beers have you had tonight?"

"Beers? No...no beers, Sir! Some guy stole my truck! Yanked me right out of the driver's side...door."

The cop stared hard at a swaying Harry, who waved his arms in frustration as the officer continued to watch him.

Satan turned behind a building and stopped short for Michael stood there, arms crossed and face devoid of amusement.

"What was that all about?"

"Lucky for Harry I was around when he got into that mishap. Your wings are a bit limp tonight Mikey, long flight?"

"Not nearly as 'limp' as your excuse, Goosie. Harry wasn't supposed to die tonight."

"I know..."

"But he was going to face a host of civil infractions."

"I know but..."

"Harry not facing these transgressions doesn't mean they didn't occur."

"I know but they weren't one of the Ten Commandments so they don't count," replied a smug Lucifer, the little flames on top of his head flaring up.

"He used the Lords name in vain."

"Big whoop! That barely rates a one on the sin-meter, Mikey."

"Even you are intelligent enough to know that both you and Harry will be under higher scrutiny."

"Yeah, yeah go preen your feathers and get out of my face," mumbled Old Scratch as he disappeared before the angels' eyes.

Michael shook his head then vanished in a silver mist. He rematerialized in front of God and gave Him his report.

"My dark counterpart seems to be a little nervous."

"Do you believe he will succeed in getting the Dean brothers into heaven, Boss?"

"My word no, Michael. Lucifer will fail because he does not have the patience to triumph and, in the end, will entertain the brothers for all eternity."

"So all of his efforts will be for naught, then."

God shrugged his shoulders wondering what Lucifer was trying to accomplish. He was expending an awful lot of energy to keep the boys out of Hell. He had something else up his sleeves and the Lord needed to find out what that was.

~

Satan rested his chin in one hand while drumming the top of his desk with the other. Two days had gone by since Harry's accident. Lucifer was watching Harry on the screen explaining to the cops how the same individual they had been pursuing that night had stolen his truck. Harry struggled to keep the pained look off his face; Rex stood stoically next to his brother. Harry favored his arm, the painful throbbing no longer deadened by the alcohol coursing through his veins. It hadn't helped matters much that he banged it getting out of the car. Harry received fifteen stitches, his explanation of having tripped in his garage and fallen onto a board full of nails falling on skeptical ears. The doctor had raised an eyebrow at him but said nothing.

Harry wanted nothing more than to hurry the procedure up but the cop behind the desk was meticulous in his questioning.

"So you're telling me that you parked your truck with the keys in the ignition in front of Bay's Bar for only a minute or two?"

"Yes, sir."

"Not the kind of neighborhood you want to do that in."

"No sir, that was a stupid thing to do."

"Who were you going inside to see?"

"A friend of mine, sir."

"Does this *friend* have a name?"

"Tom Anders, sir," replied Harry. He would have to call Tom the minute he got out of the station and tell him he was his alibi. In the meantime, the aching in his arm began to increase exponentially, the pain worming its way down into his gut.

"Anders," repeated the cop as he jotted down his name, "does he have a phone number?"

"Yes, sir, but I don't know it off the top of my head." *Hurry up you clown!*

"Do you know?" the officer addressed Rex. The cop carefully looked over the man with the slicked back light brown hair and blue eyes.

"No, sir," replied Rex while scratching at his slight paunch.

"Why were you going to see him?" The policeman turned his attention back to Harry.

"I owed him some money. Saw his car parked in front of the bar so I ran in, sir."

"So you decided to pop in real quick and give it to him while leaving your truck running out in front?"

"Yes, sir."

"Funny how your prints were the only ones found in your truck."

"It's my truck, sir. Maybe the thief wore gloves."

Lucifer slapped his forehead in exasperation.

"Al Dinaro is a two bit thug with one brain cell that is in suspended animation. It would never occur to him to wear a pair of gloves to commit a crime."

"I'm sorry, sir, I don't know what to say except that what I've told you is the truth." The agony wound its way into the pit of his stomach making Harry nauseous. He began to pale a bit as tiny beads of perspiration formed on his forehead.

"Not feeling well?" he asked.

"No, sir. I think I'm getting a cold or something."

"You're not going to puke on my clean floor, are you?"

"I think I just need a little air, sir."

"All right then. Call me with Mr. Anders' phone number. Ask for Officer Gallagher."

"Thank you, sir," replied Harry, wincing with every step back to Rex' car. He waited until Rex drove around the corner before calling Tom. Rex headed for Mackie's, their favorite watering hole a couple of blocks up the road.

"Yeah...Tom..."

"*Harry! What the hell happened the other night?*" Tom's nasally voice sounded even shriller on the cell.

"I'll tell ya later. I need you..."

"*Grady saw you near Bay's...said you was shit-faced and steered your truck into the Washburn Building!*"

"Yeah...listen up..."

"*Grady said your arm got messed up pretty bad.*"

"That's why I'm callin' you, asshole, so shut up and..."

"*You get stitches?*"

"Listen...no-shut the hell up, asshole. I saw your car in front of Bay's and was going in to give you the money I owed you."

"*How much money?*"

"Never mind how much!"

"*They're gonna ask me that you jerk!*"

"I don't know...a hundred bucks, okay?"

"*Yeah. Cool.*"

"Before I could give it to you all hell broke loose and my truck got stolen."

"*So you never gave me the money.*"

"No!"

"*Don't jump all over my shit-I'm doing you a favor!*"

15

"Yeah. Fine. Don't screw this up when they call you."

Rex pulled up next to Mackie's while Harry made another phone call.

"Officer Gallagher, please. Yeah... I'll hold."

Lucifer shook his head as the brothers entered the bar. Why bother going through all of this aggravation? Why not just simply wall them off at the very edge of Hell? Out of sight...out of earshot...out of mind. The devil watched as Harry leered at a scantily dressed woman walking into Mackie's Bar. Harry popped a pain pill and went in with his brother.

Old Gooseberry squeezed his eyes shut and shuddered.

Wednesday ~ Late Afternoon

God and Lucifer met once more but not in the abandoned warehouse, standing instead upon the dike protecting New Bedford harbor about a month after Harry's accident. A few fishermen cast their lines into the ocean while standing on the dike, enjoying each other's company almost as much as catching the blues that ran well this time of year. A clear, bright blue sky seemed to illuminate the calm sea where nary a ripple broke the surface. Gulls wheeled and squawked overhead anticipating the return of the fishing boats steaming from the fishing grounds to the northeast. This summer day bordered on perfection, a fact that seemed to beam off the Lord's contented face. He glanced over at Lucifer who lavishly spread suntan lotion all over his exposed skin. His wide straw hat and mirrored sunglasses were items a tourist wouldn't even dare to wear. Michael lifted an amused brow at him then briefly locked eyes with God.

"Beautiful day," stated the Archangel inhaling the tangy salt air. He looked across the water toward Fairhaven. A crane pulled a fishing boat out of the water at a repair dock; church spires rose up from a canopy of maple trees and two men loaded up a Boston whaler with coolers, fishing poles and other supplies. He turned around and viewed New Bedford's historic section. The Whaling Museum and the Seamen's Bethel sat perched on top of Johnny Cake Hill, portions of both buildings visible from where they stood.

"This was one of your better creations, Boss."

"I agree, Michael."

"Wasn't that bottle full when you first arrived?" asked Michael as the farting sounds of air and lotion trying to escape the same small hole filled the air.

"UV rays," stated the Devil.

"I believe those were one of your creations," clarified Michael who lifted his face to the warmth of the suns' rays.

"Isn't vanity one of your sins?" muttered Lucifer, ignoring the dig as he finished spreading the lotion onto his skin.

"I prefer to call it 'appreciation'," replied the Archangel with a grin.

"What do you want, Lucifer?" God asked calmly.

"How much atonement would Harry and Rex have to do before they can get into your house?"

"They would have to live at least another lifetime."

"I see. Can't they perform one big or good deed instead?"

"I would consider it if they managed to create world peace, Lucifer."

"Is that all? Well why didn't you say so in the first place?"

"All you had to do was ask."

"C'mon, G: a little mercy over here."

God studied the Prince of Darkness, the current of urgency inciting the flames on top of his head. They flared up and began to feed on the straw hat, sending black wisps of smoke up through the crown. God placed his hand over his mouth to stifle a laugh when the Devil started sniffing the air around him.

"Lucifer, your hat is on fire."

"Oh, shit," he yanked the blazing sun-hat off and doused it in the harbor.

"If Harry and Rex can refrain from any dubious actions

and perform one unselfish act I will gladly let them in. You can use any of your minor demons to help you."

"For how long?"

"Three days."

"Can we discuss that world peace thing again, G?" Satan asked after a long pause.

"The choice is up to you. By the way, woe unto you if even one innocent perishes during your endeavors—understand?"

Three days? *Both* Harry and Rex doing one noble deed? The Prince of Darkness already felt the weight of the task pressing down upon his bony shoulders. An army of his minions would be worn out with that daunting task! The brothers didn't even intentionally look for things to get into. Well, most of the time, anyway.

"No cheating allowed, Lucifer."

"Memory loss?"

"No."

"An affliction that requires a great deal of medication?"

"Absolutely not."

"This is most unfair!"

"You reap what you sow," Michael reminded him.

Lucifer bit his lower lip while processing the undertaking within his mind. *Those two spend most of their days humping, drinking and sleeping...the odds might just be in my favor.*

"Well?" asked the Lord.

"Fine. Three days. May we start," Lucifer pulled up his sleeve and checked his jewel encrusted platinum watch, "now?"

"The challenge ends at six p.m. on Saturday."

That world peace thing was more attainable than keeping the brothers out of trouble. Well, if he was unsuccessful in keeping them out of his house he could revert to sealing them into one of the caverns. A slow smile grew on Satan's face for he would be sure to find a suitable roommate for each for all of eternity. He disappeared into a red mist leaving God and Michael to mull over Old Gooseberry's dilemma.

"I can't remember him being this involved," said the Archangel, "at least not since the early twentieth century."

"And that was to get people *in*—not to keep them *out*."

"How much of a threat could Harry and his cohorts really be, Boss?"

"They would be harmless in Heaven, Michael, because most of their dubious traits would be stripped from them prior to entering the Pearly Gates. The reverse would be true if they were to enter Hell. Indeed, their precarious qualities would become magnified if they headed south and those very characteristics are their tickets into getting into Hell."

"But...."

"It's those bonds of hatred and insecurity that will feed the Dean clan throughout eternity, Michael."

"What if they are separated in Hell, Boss?"

"Just knowing that the others are nearby would be enough to fuel that animosity, Michael."

"I suddenly feel sorry for Goosie, Boss."

God nodded once.

~

During the time that God and Lucifer settled on their agreement, Harry walked into a dealership and purchased a brand new truck with the insurance check. It was bigger, faster and had more accessories than his destroyed vehicle. Harry sat in the driver's seat, and turned the ignition over. The motor growled to life as he sat enveloped in the new car smell, pushing button after button on the console. The radio played rock, talk, classical and a multitude of other stations in quick succession until Harry had enough and turned it off. He spent several minutes adjusting his seat then flipped the visor up and down. The passenger side door opened.

"Yo, Bro. Let's break this bitch in right."

"Hang on to your shorts."

Harry shifted into 'drive', held the brake down with his left foot and gunned the engine with his right. The truck fishtailed several times then shot out of the dealership parking lot leaving yards of rubber behind. They drove over the bridge into New Bedford, the fish processing plants clinging to the edges of the piers stretching away to either side. They followed the road until it looped around underneath the overpass, the ice plant to their left and route eighteen to their right. Harry and Rex headed for a cement block building with bars on the windows and a nameless sign hanging over the door. Harry parked the wrong way on the one-way street.

"How much extra did you get, Bro?"

"Two grand."

"Freakin' excellent." Rex opened the door to the bar, the

vacuum drawing out a cloud of cigarette smoke. "You're buying."

Harry walked in and sat at a table to the left of the entrance. He lit a cigarette and watched his brother order at the bar. A few minutes later Rex, carrying two glasses, sat down beside Harry.

"I only got time for one."

"You gonna hook up with Sherry, Bro?"

"Yeah. I haven't got laid since last night."

Rex looked at his watch. "Drop me off at the apartment on your way over to her house?"

Harry drained his glass and rose from the chair. The brothers walked out of the dimly lit bar, squinting as soon as the door opened. Harry drove back over the bridge, taking a left by the high school. He drove up to their apartment building, parked and nodded at Rex.

"Don't wait up."

"I won't, Bro."

~

Harry couldn't wait to see Sherry. He pulled up to her tenement and climbed up to the third floor, grinning as she stood in the doorway waiting for him. A thin woman with large breasts, she wore her thick blond hair up in a ponytail. A red silk robe hugged her curves.

"Hi baby!"

"Hi yourself."

Harry held her close, his tongue probing her tonsils while his manhood stiffened in his jeans. They maneuvered into the apartment, Sherry closing the door with her foot. After several long moments, they separated and headed for the bedroom.

The sun began its descent when Harry emerged from the bedroom, the sound of running water coming from the bathroom. He grabbed a soda from the refrigerator then sat down in front of the television. Surfing through the channels, he stopped and watched a baseball game. The Red Sox were up by three runs and it was only the bottom of the first inning. He turned the volume up when Sherry dried her hair then down when she emerged from the bedroom.

"You like?"

Harry stared at the skirt hugging her hips then up at her flowered blouse, which barely contained her chest. Red lipstick, black mascara and dangly earrings completed her ensemble. She sauntered over to him and sat on his lap.

"Well?"

"I like! Let's go."

Harry drove to Mackie's, a bar notorious for dirty glasses and nightly brawls. He had a brand new truck, a vial of leftover pain meds and a girlfriend with big breasts who put out anytime or anywhere. Life was good.

They walked into the dingy bar, the lights from the neon signs advertising a variety of beers illuminating the grimy windows. Mirrors sporting more beer advertisements reflected the dim lighting hanging from the smoke-stained ceiling. Backless stools with ripped seats lined the bar; square tables surrounded by three chairs abutted the wall. The couple plopped their backsides at the bar, their drinks already waiting for them.

Harry placed one hand on Sherry's breast and belted back the shot of whiskey with the other. He noticed a guy across the bar staring at Sherry's cleavage, her breasts straining to pop the only button keeping her shirt done. Harry glared at him.

"You got a problem?" he bellowed across the bar.

"Nope."

"Quit staring at my girls' boobs!"

"They're out for everyone to see," replied the unkempt man wearing a dirty gray tee-shirt and soiled jeans. He focused his bleary gaze on Sherry's chest while making sucking motions with his mouth.

Harry slid off the barstool and walked over to the man, fists clenched and whiskey pumping through his veins.

"Your old lady ain't got any this big?"

"Hell ya," he pointed his jaw at Sherry, "but I still wanna put my lips on her nipples."

"Hey—put your mouth on this!" Harry shouted then struck the other man in the face. Blood spurted out of his nose and sprayed against the mirrored ad beside him. He bull rushed Harry pinning him against the wall.

The barmaid picked up the phone to call the police. The patrons nearest to the fighters picked up their bottles and glasses and stood against the wall, cheering and whistling as punches missed and landed. Tables were overturned, full ashtrays crashed to the floor scattering cigarette butts all over the place.

Sherry watched with a blank expression, snapping her gum and twirling her overly bleached hair around her press-on fingernails. Sherry shifted her breasts until they were millimeters from flopping out of her bra and scanned the bar for another boyfriend.

The sounds of sirens grew closer but that did not stop the blows. Bruises and welts erupted on their faces. Harry's opponent grabbed his tee shirt ripping the sleeve and collar. Harry was slightly smaller than his opponent was but that did nothing to discourage him from not backing down. The blue lights filling the windows outside the bar or the static noises from the radios as the cops ran in to stop the altercation failed to deter the fighters. Harry continued to unload punches on his adversary, heedless of the arms grappling to contain him. One of the officers recognized Harry from other violent encounters and smiled.

There is a God, he thought to himself.

The Prince of Darkness slapped the top of his desk with his hand in exasperation and disappeared, reappearing inside the bar seconds later. Old Gooseberry was not happy, a feeling that intensified when he spotted Michael in the far corner. The Archangel, visible only to Lucifer, stood with his arms crossed wearing a bemused look on his face. The devil turned and received a blow to his cheek. He stood still for a moment, the room spinning beyond his blurry sight. Old Scratch reeled into a table and slipped, landing with a thud on the floor.

"You okay, buddy?" asked a cop crouching alongside him. "Want to press charges?"

"I'm...fine and no." He glared at Harry's challenger.

Let's see how many no-no's Harry has managed to achieve in the past hour. Better yet how many will you be able to expunge, Goosie?

Old Gooseberry shot Michael a dirty look.

Screw you.

The melee was finally under control with Harry and his rival in handcuffs. Sherry succeeded in acting concerned for about two minutes before sidling up to a brawny biker who cupped one hand under her breast while drinking a beer with the other. Harry didn't see her or he would have knocked her off her barstool, cops or no cops. He let loose a barrage of swears as the tow truck came and hooked up his new truck, which was parked in a 'No Parking' zone while struggling with the officers to stop the operator from his task. It took five burly cops to get him into the back of the cruiser and buckle him in. The Prince of Darkness, his hands tied for the moment, waited for a more opportune time to get Harry out of this mess.

"Buy you a drink, buddy?" Michael asked.

"You don't drink, Mikey," he retorted but sat down anyway, his fingers dabbing at his cheek. He glanced over at Michael's crisp white shirt and neatly ironed jeans. "Nice outfit."

Michael looked at Old Scratch's faded tee shirt and wrinkled jeans. The Devil's pants sagged even while sitting down. "You really ought to work out a bit."

"Piss off."

"A little wine now and then never hurt anyone." Michael smirked as he raised his hand to catch the bartender's attention.

"Have you noticed the kind of establishment we're in? I doubt that that rusting still in the back can produce anything short of bad anti-freeze."

"Red wine, please, and a beer for my friend here," he ordered ignoring the sour look on the bartender's face.

"How are your cheeks?"

"Better than his will be."

The barmaid with the pockmarked face and frizzy hair placed a small screw top bottle of wine in front of Michael, and then deposited a glass of beer in front of the Devil. He grimaced at the lipstick marks along the rim and the greasy fingerprints along the glass. Old Scratch spotted one clean glass on the shelf and deftly maneuvered it toward him with the subtle wave of his hand. The beer disappeared from one and reappeared in the other.

"You realize, Goosie, that the more you protect and help Harry the more he'll believe he is immune to bad luck and continue to tempt fate."

"Look, Mikey, mind your own damn business." He watched the Archangel extend his pinky whenever he took a sip of wine. "And stop drinking like a girl."

"I'm sipping my wine in the way it was meant to be savored, Goosie."

"*It's out of a screw top bottle!*" he said through clenched teeth.

Michael casually glanced around the room. The men wore grubby clothing and three-day-old stubble on their faces; the women dressed in skintight clothing and layers of make-up. Michael gripped the bottle as if he were holding a beer.

"Happy now?"

"I'd be happier if you pissed off," muttered the Devil.

"Face it, Goosie," Michael drained the rest of the wine, "Harry's final address has already been established and there's nothing you can do about it. Thanks for the drink and good night." Michael abruptly departed, stiffing him for the drinks.

That bastard! The Prince of Darkness slid off the stool and headed for the door.

"Hey! You! Pay the goddamn bill or these two gorillas are gonna beat the money outta ya!" The barmaid's shrill voice cut through the smoky room.

Lucifer raised a brow then slipped out of the bar, the two men a second behind him, and evaporated into the night. The men glanced up and down the street, banging their fists into their palms as they scoured the area for the freeloader. They searched the alleyways to either side of the bar then peered into the coffee shop next door.

"The little asshole's hidin' somewheres."

"He'll be back."

"You think he's that stupid?"

"Yeah."

"Let's go, we got some cleanin' up to do."

~

No sooner did Lucifer sit in his chair when the red warning light on the monitor focused on Rex began to flash.

"What now!"

Old Gooseberry grabbed the remote and increased the volume. Rex' face was drenched in sweat, his body slamming into the blonde woman beneath him.

"C'mon! Faster!" she panted, lifting her pelvis into his thrusts.

"Myco!"

"Yes, Master?" The misshapen imp waddled over to him, his ample bulk bouncing with each step even though his many arms tried valiantly to keep it under control. Wild white hair on the top of his head and along the joints bobbed and swayed as if listening to a heavy metal band. Myco patiently waited for his task.

"Check this out."

Myco stared at the screen, tilting his head to one side as he watched the humans thrashing about on the bed. He shrugged his gaunt shoulders then looked over at the Devil.

"They are copulating, Master."

"Yes, Myco, I'm aware of that."

"This is not the first time Master has seen..."

"*Never mind.*"

"Master needs to extricate the subject from the Atwood residence before his deed is noticed."

Lucifer tenderly touched his sore cheeks, the swelling now at its greatest. "If the son of a bitch hits me I'm going to yank his intestines out through the smallest orifice on his body."

Rex shuddered several times then withdrew his member from the woman.

"That would not be through his penis, Master."

The Devil clicked off the monitor.

~

Lucifer took a deep breath outside the woman's bedroom then knocked on the window. He heard hasty movements and hurried whisperings before the bedroom door creaked open then closed with a muffled thud. A car started and began to move, the driver's side door slamming shut seconds later.

The Devil exhaled, grateful at how uneventful this situation turned out. He spun around and stared at a wall that nearly encompassed the entire neighborhood. Lucifer looked up at a swarthy man with no neck and bulging biceps. His dark hair hung in greasy strands around his bearded face; his legs were the size of trees and his chest wide enough to double as a movie screen. The man sported tiger tattoos along his shirtless chest, the tails and paws disappearing beneath his leather vest. The sour stench of sweat enveloped Lucifer like some noxious fog.

"You some sort of freakin' perv?"

"Uh…no…I'm…"

"You ain't bangin' my old lady, are ya?"

The man's wife pulled up the blinds and watched her husband deal with the intruder. She wore a blue velvet short robe but hadn't bothered to tie it yet. A pair of bargain basement implants made one nipple point north and the other one south; the wax job between her thighs looked like a crazed smiley face. She lifted the blonde wig off her head and tossed it on the crumpled sheets. She resumed watching her husband and the Devil, her jaws working on a wad of gum.

"*Not for all the souls in the world!*"

"What did you just say?" The man seized Old Scratch's

shirt with one hand and hauled him up until he was level with his face.

Snarling tigers filled the Devil's vision, their formidable fangs and imposing claws growing larger with each passing moment.

"Nice kitties?" Lucifer said in a high-pitched voice, his bony finger pointing at the roaring tiger inked onto the man's upper chest. It was the last thing he saw.

The man dropped him to the ground, leaving him moaning in the darkness. A shadow detached itself from the gloom and scooped up the fallen Devil.

"Time to go home, Goosie."

"Ungh..."

Michael chuckled.

~

"Master?"

"Uhh..."

"Master feeling better?"

"Myco? Is that you? How many pieces am I in?"

"One, Master."

Lucifer felt the cool compress across both cheeks.

"What time is it?"

"Dawn. The Dean brothers are accounted for."

"I hate them."

"Yes, Master."

"I truly hate them."

"Does Master feel like sitting up and having a cup of coffee?"

"'Master' prefers lying here in a pool of his own self pity and," a scab opened on his swollen lips releasing a warm, metallic tasting liquid, "blood."

"It would be less painful and exasperating to welcome them into your realm, Master."

"What? Are you insane?" Lucifer bolted upright, the damp cloth dropping into his lap. He abruptly clutched his head, rocking back and forth to stop the epic sword fight taking place within his cranium. He accepted the cup from Myco then waved him away.

Lucifer sipped his coffee and stared out into the main room. Adolph's eyes blazed with fury as the holy man rolled up the Torah. He nodded condescendingly at the dictator's muffled outrage while reverently stowing the precious object in his case. Myco wobbled up to the holy man, spoke briefly with him then guided him out of the chamber. Old Gooseberry sighed and sought his chair, grabbing the clicker as he sat down.

The Prince of Darkness flipped through the channels. Bowling? No. Presidential debates? *Hmm...I must add this one to my list of agonizing tortures.* Sitcom? Un-uh. News?

"Here are the top news headlines," read the newscaster with perfectly coiffed hair and wearing an Ann Taylor suit. "Four people were arrested on drug charges when local and state police raided a warehouse on East Central Street. Yesterday's rollover on Sconticut Neck Road is still under investigation. Alcohol seems to have been a factor in that lunchtime accident. Police are on the lookout for a peeping Tom in the east end of town…"

"What I saw is *still* giving *me* nightmares!" He turned off the television and readjusted the compress, holding it in place with one hand while drinking his coffee with the other.

Thursday Morning

Old Gooseberry emerged from one of the tunnels leaving behind the petty sinners, their screams eliciting a smile on his thin features. They amused him on occasion, especially when he made an unexpected stop and personally tormented them. He couldn't ignore them even if their sins were inconsequential compared to the heavyweights in the main chamber: that would be just plain wrong. He took the list from a patiently waiting Myco, read it over then signed it before handing it back to him. He watched the deformed imp shuffle away, his cotton candy like hair bouncing erratically with every step. For a few, brief precious moments Satan's realm was as it should be. He watched a minor demon approach Myco, the low-ranking fiend keeping his eyes averted from Myco as he passed on his report. Myco suddenly jiggled toward him, the faster than normal pace an ominous sign.

"The Dean Brothers are at the swap meet, Master."

"And?"

"Sherry, the Atwood couple and Harry's ex-girlfriend Debbie are there as well."

"Debbie…Debbie…" Lucifer rubbed his chin, the little flames dancing on his head. "Not the Debbie who stole her dying grandmother's jewelry then sold it so she could go to Vegas for a week?"

"The same, Master."

"Nice."

~

Michael had to admit he enjoyed watching Lucifer work so

diligently to keep someone out of his residence. What Harry couldn't win over from someone, Rex would steal. The Archangel could picture the brothers breaking into Satan's office, their feet on his desk, drinking his precious Scotch and smoking his expensive cigars while watching some tawdry daytime talk program. They'd laugh at the pathetic lives on the screen swearing and fighting over the stupidest things, never realizing that those people mirrored their own lives. When that show concluded they would flip to some court program and make fun of the fools that got their comeuppance for their greed and stupidity. The brothers' mantra was 'never get caught but if you do make sure the bullshit smells like the sweetest of roses'.

"You look terrible, Goosie," Michael greeted the Devil at the gates of the flea market.

"Screw you."

"Beautiful day, isn't it?" Michael glanced to the right toward the approaching Atwood's then over to the left where Sherry and Debbie were just getting out of their car. Harry and Rex strolled past tables full of tools a few rows in from the parking lot.

"What part of 'screw you' don't you understand?"

Michael grinned at him then winked at a couple of young women who took their sweet time in scrutinizing every square inch of his body.

"Careful, Mikey… vanity is frowned down upon."

The Archangel laughed as he slapped the Devil on his back. "Good luck today. I'll be around in case you need me."

Old Scratch scowled at Michael's retreating form, wishing he could make his own scrawny body fill out a pair of jeans the way the Archangel did.

"Oh shit!" Old Gooseberry darted behind the large 'Flea Market Today' sign just before Jon and China Atwood sauntered by, snickering as China's left nipple watched Jon while her right one pointed to the ground. He'd have to be careful or it'll take more than cold compresses and coffee to fix him up next time Jon got a hold of him. His powers were, after all, limited in the land of the living.

Rex bought a bunch of rusty name brand tools. He paid twenty dollars for three screwdrivers, a couple of vise grips, four hammers and two crescent wrenches.

"You gonna stop off at the mall on the way back?"

"Yeah," Rex patted the paper bag. "I'm gonna get credit for 'em at the store then I'll head over to the branch in Fairhaven and get my money for 'em."

"You're gonna get caught, Bro."

"Nah, besides, they're the ones who advertise a 'lifetime' guarantee."

"How much you think you're gonna get?"

"Two hundred, maybe two hundred fifty bucks."

"Good deal."

"Yeah."

"You're buying dinner."

Rex grinned then his gaze strayed to a table loaded with more tools a few booths over. He took his bag and left Harry to poke through a stack of old car posters.

Old Scratch walked past a booth manned by a fat man selling small bottles of blue liquid. A hairy arm reached out to catch Old Gooseberry's attention.

"Are you vexed by the Evil One?"

The Devil focused on the man, the strands of gray hair swirled around the top of his head held in place by the man's perspiration. His beefy hand pointed to the bottles.

"Keep the Evil One at bay for only five bucks."

"This," Satan picked up one of the containers, "is going to protect me from the Devil? What's in it?"

"I can't tell you what the ingredients are," the flabby man whispered in secretive tones, "but rest assured it works."

"Really?"

"I guarantee it."

Old Gooseberry sighed and slowly shook his head. "Have you ever seen the Evil One?"

The man leaned closer to the Devil. "Once."

"What did he look like?"

"He was hideous…all teeth and horns…cloven feet and tiny wings!"

Old Gooseberry's eyes narrowed, the man's insults rattling around in his mind. "Does this look cloven to you?" The seller took a step backward as Old Scratch lifted his foot onto his table.

"Get that off my table! Look, I'll tell you what, my friend, buy one and I'll throw in a free bottle."

A tic sprouted up on Satan's jaw.

"It works against vampires, zombies and ACLU lawyers, too. Whaddya say, buddy?"

Old Gooseberry walked away ignoring the man's continued attempts to get him to buy the colored water.

Lucifer followed the brothers for hours all the while avoiding Jon and his wife. Neither Rex nor China had noticed each other all morning until the brothers and the Atwood couple rounded the same row and almost bumped into one another. Rex kept his composure until China stealthily fondled his crotch as she walked by. She accompanied her husband toward a booth full of car parts.

"Horizontal friend of yours, Bro?"

"Yup."

"Ain't you worried about her old man?"

"Nah. Big guys like that can't wipe their own ass."

"You almost done picking through this garbage?" asked Harry.

"Yeah."

"Good. Let's grab a soda and a sandwich on the way back."

"Aw…shit."

"What?"

"Debbie and Sherry are heading this way."

The dim lighting in the bar was a perfect backdrop for Sherry's bleached hair and pancake make-up but daylight was not her friend. Pale skin and dark circles under her eyes topped by a bland mane gave her a sickly appearance. Breasts that strained to pop out of her push-up bra now flopped unfettered beneath a loose tank top.

Debbie fared little better. Her long reddish hair framed a

gaunt face; her threadlike eyebrows seemed to recoil from her calculating brown eyes.

"Hey, Sherry! Look who's here! Asshole number one *and* two."

"Screw you, Debbie!" Harry spat at her.

"No thanks...I gave up weenie dogs for Lent."

"Lent was months ago, stupid."

"And I still don't miss the weenie dog."

"What, you doing this rag now?" Harry pointed at Sherry. "What's the matter? Ain't no guy able to satisfy you after screwing me?"

"Yeah, Bro. You made her switch from the pole to the hole!" The brothers laughed and playfully pushed each other.

"At least Sherry knows how to get my rocks off."

"I hear ya, girlfriend," Sherry piped in. "Half the time I was wondering if it was even in!"

"You knew it was in, baby!" Harry's hips pumped the air in front of him. "They heard you screamin' for more all the way up in Boston."

"You got that right," Debbie slipped her arm around Sherry's waist then squeezed her ass. "We was screamin' for more because we didn't even realize your weenie dog was already in!"

The women walked away, their laughter punctuated by an occasional snort. They ignored the brothers' comments but flipped them off as they rounded a booth at the end of the row.

"Bro?"

"Ya?"

"You think them two is getting it on?" asked Rex.

Harry imagined the two women naked in bed beside him performing all sorts of kinky acts. Both wanted him to satisfy them individually and ignore the other. Harry grinned as they pushed each other away from him before the shoving began in earnest. He got up from the bed, lit a cigarette and watched the women fist fight for his attention.

"Bro?"

"Nah," replied Harry, rubbing his crotch.

Old Gooseberry breathed a sigh of relief as the women walked away. His respite was short lived as a booming voice rippled across the field.

"Hey! It's the perv!"

The Devil spun around looking for the source. He spotted Jon Atwood two aisles over. A faint whimper escaped the Prince of Darkness' throat before his legs awoke and transported him to the edge of the flea market near the parking lot. He sidled up behind a tree, peeking around it to mark Atwood's whereabouts. The giant man raced up and down the lines of cars, occasionally dropping to his knees to check underneath them. Satisfied that his prey had escaped, he gripped China's arm and headed back toward the stalls.

Michael cocked his head as he watched Harry walk past a man selling balloons, the green, blue, red and yellow spheres tethered to his cart with bright strings. Four children wearing washed out shorts and shirts stared with an anticipatory joy at the cheerful globes. Their mother pushed a stroller past them, her tired features and rough hands matching her dull clothing.

"Momma? Can we have a balloon?"

"Yeah, Momma! I want a pretty red one!" the smallest child, a little girl with short brown hair squealed.

"No…not today, kids."

"Pleeaassseee!" they shouted in unison.

The mother continued on, too weary to reply.

Harry wandered over to the balloon vendor.

"How much for four?"

"Ten bucks."

"Ten bucks for a little bit of rubber and air?"

"I gotta make a living, too, guy."

"Here," he shoved the money into the seller's hand, "gimme one of each color."

Harry followed the family then called over the oldest kid, a skinny boy overloaded with freckles. The boy stared suspiciously at him.

"Here…"

"What do I gotta do for 'em?"

"Nothin'."

"You don't get somethin' for nothin', Mister."

"Take the damn things or I'll let 'em go."

The boy guardedly closed the distance between them and took the balloons, then ran to catch up with his mother.

Harry watched her chastise him for taking things from a stranger then handed one to each of her children. They jumped up and down, their laughter echoing back to where Harry stood. Their mother looked at him for a brief second before urging the giggling caravan on.

"Someone is looking out for you today," Michael stated as he caught up with the Prince of Darkness.

"I can do this on my own, Mikey."

"Right. So I take it you won't be needing my help?"

"Why would I need your help, Mikey?"

The Archangel nodded in the direction of the parking lot where Rex and Harry had stopped in front of a shabby van. Whether or not he was truly considered necessary remained to be seen but Michael wasn't about to let Satan relax for even a single moment. Besides, the panicked expression on Satan's face promised at least some amusement and besides, Michael still had a half bag of popcorn to finish. He made his way to a nearby bench and sat down to watch the action.

Rex and Harry walked around the vehicle, its rusting sides in stark contrast to the fancy chrome hubcaps. It used to be a deep red color but continual modifications had left it a dull brick shade. There were numerous stickers on the back windows; so many in fact that it was nearly impossible to see through the brightly colored shapes.

"Isn't this Eli's van?" asked Rex.

"Yeah. The jerk owes me money," replied Harry.

"You gave Eli money? What's wrong with you, Bro? You know that he never pays anyone back."

"Yeah, I know but I figured that unlike the other suckers he took for a ride at least I've got the balls to get it back," he said peeking in the window.

"What's he got in there?" asked Rex.

"A pile of dirty clothes, some empty boxes and a bunch of

empty beer cans.

"That's it?" asked Rex as he shifted his package to his other arm.

"That's it."

"You want to wait for him?"

"Yeah. I need a cigarette break. We can wait and watch for him in the shade," he said walking over to a broad maple tree a few yards away.

They had bought sodas on the way out and proceeded to sit and drink while waiting for Eli.

"There's Eli," said Rex as the wiry man came around to the drivers' side of the van. Eli froze for an instant then desperately tried to get into his van before the brothers came over but dropped his keys and lost his chance to escape.

"What's going on, Eli?" asked Harry leaning against the driver side door. He crushed his cigarette beneath his boot heel.

"Nothin'." Eli's sweat ran down the side of his cheeks and landed on his shirt collar. Harry and Rex sneered at the abstract designs on his shirt and thought how hideous it looked, especially the gaudy shades of yellows and greens.

"Where's my money, candy ass?"

"I'll get it to you tomorrow…I promise, Harry."

"You'll give me whatever you have now."

"I need it…you know…food for my kids."

"Here, Bro," said Rex as he deftly plucked Eli's wallet from his jeans' pocket and handed it over to Harry. Harry took out sixty bucks and shoved it into his pocket before throwing the wallet onto the ground. Eli's shirt grew darker with perspiration as he stood motionless in front of the brothers. Soon the only reservoir of liquid was in his bladder.

"You bring me the other hundred and forty tonight or I'll hunt you down and beat the shit out of you, got it?"

"Yeah, sure thing Harry. Tonight."

"You sure you ain't got nothing else?" demanded Rex eyeballing the envelope sticking up from Eli's shirt pocket. Before Eli could react Rex yanked it out and opened it, the smile on his face growing broader with every passing second.

"Those aren't mine!" protested Eli without moving a single muscle in his body except from the neck up.

"You got that right!" replied Rex as he triumphantly held up a pair of Pats tickets to the season opener on the fifty-yard line. Someone sure liked him today to put these puppies in his hands. Rex closed his eyes. He could smell the steaks cooking in Gillette Stadium's parking lot, hear the shouts from the stands and feel the power of the players as they battled on the gridiron. The grass would be bright green, the sky a brilliant blue and the beer ice cold in his hand as the wide receiver broke free from the safeties and raced to the end zone.

"Mackie's. Tonight." Harry poked Eli's bony chest with a finger.

Eli could barely keep his hands from shaking as he fumbled with his keys to get into his van and far away from these two bullies. Rex was still 'watching' the game and it took Harry several moments to break into Rex' reverie, which ended abruptly when a defender knocked the ball loose on the one yard line.

"Shit!" stated Rex bitterly.

"What?" asked Harry.

"He fumbled the freakin' ball!"

"Who?" demanded Harry, staring hard at his brother.

"Never mind," he replied then walked back to Harry's car with him.

The Devil and the Angel watched the confrontation end, the former relieved that it was an insignificant shakedown.

"See? You didn't even have to go over there!" remarked Michael with some measure of levity.

"Good-bye, Mikey," the Devil stated as he strode away only to find the Archangel keeping pace with him. Well, where he was going the Angel was certainly not going to follow, although he would do just about anything to get Michael onto his turf. He could punish the Angel by sealing him up in the same corridor as with Harry and the rest of his annoying group. How sweet would that be?

"How are the two new arrivals?" asked the Archangel.

"The brothers?"

"Yes."

"They're waiting for their virgins: the dumb asses haven't figured out that only bad girls end up in Hell."

"You could pretend they'll show up any day," offered Michael with a little smirk.

"That's not nice, Mikey!"

"Neither is Hell…no offense meant."

"None taken."

Lucifer tried not to imagine what Heaven was like for the mere thought of all that whiteness, lightness, and politeness was giving him the heebie-jeebies. Heaven's calm airiness and benevolent demeanors would be his ultimate end: death by extreme boredom. He shivered involuntarily at the mere thought of feeling a fluffy cloud under his butt as he sat on it holding his chin in his hand and having no one to vex. Any nasty comment he'd throw at anyone would be met with a condescending look or an understanding little nod. Satan felt his stomach turn and quickly filled his mind with visions of Hell and his dark yet sumptuous office.

"Have I told you how much I dislike you?" asked Satan as he stopped and faced Michael. The angel didn't flinch and Lucifer realized he would see the Archangels face day in and day out forever. *For freakin' ever!*

"I think I lost count at about eight or nine times."

"We'll make it an even ten then: *Get out of my face!*" The little flames on top of the Devils' head burned more brightly, crackling with contempt for the Archangel who seemed nonplussed by his smoldering impatience. Michael simply smiled at him then disappeared into thin air.

Cheeky bastard.

Thursday ~ 6 p.m.

Eli met Harry at Mackie's that night but he did more than come to give him the money. Harry had roughed up too many people and many of them wanted nothing more than to return the favor. Harry was a strapping man with few apprehensions about taking someone, anyone, on regardless of size or disposition. Fully aware of Harry's capabilities and stubborn refusal to back away, Eli brought a small army with him. The frizzy haired bartender scrutinized the men wandering in with Eli, their furtive glances and abrupt whisperings arousing her suspicion. She frowned when Harry, Rex and a couple of their friends entered the seedy bar. Eli walked over to them, his friends watching the meeting in the mirror behind the bar.

"Where's my freakin' money?" demanded Harry.

"I got your money right here." Eli reached into his back pocket and pulled out a plain brown wrapper, watching as Harry opened it and counted out the bills.

"There's only a hundred here. You owe me forty more, you little shit."

"I ain't gonna give you the rest."

"You're not what?"

"I ain't got it but my friend over there does."

Harry stared at Eli for a second then glanced over his shoulder toward the bar. He turned back to Eli only to find his fist against his cheek.

The ensuing melee erupted so instantaneously that the bartender stared at the chaos for several long seconds before picking up the phone and calling the cops. She ducked several times as glasses and bottles whistled near her head and crashed into the mirror behind her, the noise so loud it was hard for her to speak let alone for the dispatcher to hear. Bodies collided with each other. Tables and chairs overturned. Pool cues became Louisville sluggers; the dull whacking sounds indicating more than one home run had been hit.

Seeing that the turmoil was distracting everyone in the place Rex sneaked behind the bar and into the cooler in the back. He slinked out the rear door carrying cases of booze and depositing them in the back of his truck. He always insisted on parking near the back door for easy getaways and even easier takeaways for, in his mind, the bar could afford losing a bottle or two.

"That's what insurance is for," muttered Rex as he slid the last case of beer onto the bed of his truck.

He spotted the blue lights quickly closing in on their block and ran back in to get Harry, bowling over the barmaid in the process. He grabbed his brother by the arm and yanked him out the back, the bartender pushed against the ice machine for the second time in thirty seconds.

"You son of a bitch! I'll kick you right in your…"

Rex slammed the door shut, her tirade effectively silenced.

Harry steadied himself with one hand on the gray dashboard, his bloody handprint smearing to the right as Rex took a corner too quickly. Droplets of blood spattered against the window when Harry jerked his head to the side.

"Hey! Quit bleeding all over the place, Bro!"

"I can't help it! Hey! What's that clinking sound?" asked Harry.

"Beer bottles."

"I thought you took back your empties the other day?"

"They got refilled tonight."

Harry grinned. "Did you get any whiskey?"

"I only found three bottles, Bro…what the hell!" Rex slammed on his brakes as a shadow detached itself from the curb and halted in front of the truck. A string of obscenities burst from Harry's mouth as he hit the dashboard. A pair of bloody handprints and a strand of red drool appeared on the console as he tried to brace himself from adding any more injuries to himself. Rex glared at him. Already angry because of the mess in his cab, Rex got out of his truck in a huff and walked up to the idiot that ran out in front of his vehicle.

"Hey! Guys! The cops saw you take off and the barmaid knows that you stole the beer!" stated the Devil. He heard an unmistakable chuckle from the darkened recess behind him. *Just once I'd like to work without an audience!*

"Get the hell out of the way you asshole!" roared Harry from inside the truck, his left eye beginning to close.

"No, really!"

"Listen, asshole," growled Rex, "if you don't get the hell out of my way I'm gonna knock you on your ass!"

"I'm only trying to…" Lucifer dropped to the ground as a swirling galaxy of the most nauseating colors filled his sight, his eyes watering so badly he couldn't even see the truck taking off. It took a few seconds for the pain to kick in. "…help you."

"You okay, Goosie?" came a voice then a hand that helped him back up onto his feet. Too stunned to trade barbs with the Angel, Old Gooseberry allowed Michael to lead him to the dark entrance and sit him down on the stoop.

"That insignificant, arrogant, meaningless little mortal just punched me in my nose, Mikey."

"I saw." Michael could barely contain himself, wiping away the tears of silent laughter running down his well-chiseled cheeks.

"That freakin' idiot punched me...*me*! *Satan*!"

"I don't think he knew who he was slugging, Goosie, for even those two would know better than to hit the Prince of Darkness." The Archangel found it difficult to breathe for the look on Lucifer's face was priceless. It ran the gamut of emotions from shock to anger in a matter of seconds. The Devils' broken nose and bruised cheeks prevented any more sentiments from scampering across his countenance. When Satan regained his composure there would be, well, Hell to pay.

Michael, please stop tormenting him.

The Lord sent the silent command into the Archangels' mind. Michael obeyed even though the temptation to keep giving the Devil a taste of his own medicine was overwhelming. God and Satan had battled each other over eternity with but one rule: never kick the other when he was down. The Prince of Darkness had, for the moment, met his match -a mortal no less—and deserved a chance to regain his self-respect.

"C'mon, Goosie: I'll walk you almost all the way home."

Michael stopped at the Gates of Hell and handed Satan over to Myco. The demon collected the muttering Devil in his many arms and gazed down upon the newest injury. He glanced up at the Archangel.

"Harry?"

"No, the broken nose is compliments of Rex."

"Master will be very angry when he wakes up."

"Patch him up, Myco, Master still has another thirty hours or so of keeping watch over the Dean brothers."

"Thank you, Michael."

"Good night, Myco."

The Gates of Hell slammed shut leaving Michael rolling with laughter on the other side. It took several long minutes before the Archangel could collect himself enough to fly back up to Heaven.

Myco carried Lucifer through a side door and down an unused hall. He sat Old Scratch in his chair, tilting his head back to stem the bleeding that had started once more. The portly imp gingerly placed a bag of ice over Old Gooseberry's face, the chill gradually reviving him. He stood unobtrusively by his master, patiently waiting for any order.

Lucifer opened his eyes, the room a fusion of brown and silver. The memories of what had transpired earlier this evening came flooding back carrying with it a torrent of anger. The flames on his head shot upward, burning with unabated fury.

"Myco, which tunnel is the most awful?"

"Section seven, area thirty-four, Master," replied the demon in his wheezy tone as he took a few steps away from the raging inferno. His bloodshot eyes gazed adoringly at the Devil while his many hands flickered with movement as he sought to make his Master's current predicament more comfortable. He placed a cold glass of water within Lucifer's easy reach then positioned a pillow behind his neck to ease the strain of leaning back.

"Who's in there now?" He would try to avoid letting the Dean group into his realm but it was prudent to plan ahead nonetheless.

"Incubus is entertaining an assemblage of child molesters in that section, Master."

"Dammit! The next worst underground passage?" Satan was not about to let them move up the ladder even if it was to make room for the Deans.

"Section nine, area three, Master."

"And who occupies that burrow?"

"Liars posing as spiritual leaders who fleeced the poor and downtrodden of their last pennies and hopes, Master."

"Okay," Satan gently shifted the bag of ice, "we'll use that one if need be."

"Master, where shall the liars go if that happens?"

"Put them in with Incubus for a spell, that way they'll know what getting screwed up the ass without Vaseline is all about." Satan suddenly began to feel a little better proving that work did indeed take the edge off a bad day. He noticed Myco staring at him, the imp's eyes full of concern.

"What?"

"Master just…" he began but could not finish his sentence.

"'Master' what, Myco?"

"Master just had a pang of compassion for those who were cheated," he said in a whisper fearing the Devil's reaction to such a bold remark. He waited for Master to explode with fury, the clumps of hair on his bulbous head vibrating with his nervousness.

Lucifer opened his mouth to offer the demon a stinging retort then realized that Myco was right. He hadn't been thinking about Incubus' gratification but of the liars getting their due for swindling the fools who had put their faith in them. Was he getting soft? Had his mean streak hit a speed bump? Had Michael somehow tainted him? No. It had to have been the blow to his face. Yes. That was it: the punch to his nose was the reason.

"Master will have quite the headache before too long," Myco stated quietly hoping to change the subject.

"I already have one, Myco," he replied as the dull throbbing began to assert itself in his head. Being evil came naturally and often had immediate rewards, but being good? What had that landed him? A broken nose and sudden pity for the downtrodden. Lucifer abruptly felt sorry for himself, the expression visible on his face.

"Perhaps another slap on the back of Adolph's head will make Master feel better?" suggested Myco, noting the downcast look. Lucifer didn't respond prompting Myco to leave him alone for a while. The Prince of Darkness sighed heavily then stared without seeing at the suffering occurring beyond his office window. After a while, his eyes became swollen slits leaving him no other recourse but to recline his chair and fall into a fitful sleep...

...Lucifer emerged from his office to find himself completely alone. He did not hear the Rabbi reading from the Torah nor did he see Adolph tied to the chair. Jeffrey, Vlad and Idi

were nowhere within sight. Silence reigned. The sulphurous fumes were replaced with thick cigarette smoke while the rivers of lava burped air once or twice before they, too, became still. He called out for Myco but the imp didn't respond nor did any of the other demons he summoned. Then he heard the muted sounds of something grating yet squishy approaching from one of the tunnels.

The oozing and scraping became louder, and the closer it came to the mouth of the cave, the more apprehensive Satan became. The scuffing sounds grew as if caused by some huge form unable to move its bulk more than at a snails' pace. Nervous and perplexed, Satan shifted on his spindly legs while his head flames cowered against his skull. There were noises issuing from the unseen thing but they were so irrational that he could not identify a single sound. It neared the last bend in the tunnel and the devil could see the massive shadow of a blob-like thing with swaying tentacles raised high overhead. He quickly ran through the roster in his mind but could not remember having such a creature in his kingdom. The sounds, however, began to take on individual tones and what he heard made his skin crawl.

"Kiss my ass you jerk!"

"Up yours asshole!"

"Where's my freakin' money?"

"Don't bleed in my truck!"

Satan stood rooted in place, his chest unable to rise and fall as he waited for his nightmare to exit the tunnel and plant itself firmly in his house. It rounded the last bend and emerged from the tunnel. The thing stood nearly twenty feet high with over a dozen heads that bobbed and turned on their appendages. Harry, Rex, Sherry, Debbie and the Atwood's shrieked and swore at one another with a vengeance they could not have achieved in life. Spittle rained down on Lucifer as the monster hovered overhead like some harbinger of doom and all Satan could muster was an ineffective choked cry of ruin.

"Hey asshole! Where's the freakin' booze?" Rex screeched down at him.

"Quit moving around, bitch! I wanna bite your freakin' head!" howled Harry at Debbie.

"Watch out for his weenie dog!" Sherry screeched.

The Prince of Darkness' jaw dropped. The chaos that erupted from this monstrosity exploded into every corner of his realm making escape impossible. The other souls called out to the Dean Clan, egging them on in shrill voices. Lucifer finally broke free from the terrible trance. Scouring Hell for some sort of weapon to destroy this monstrosity with, the Devil found a sword. He lifted it up and sliced through one of the tentacles supporting Harry's head. The head fell to the ground and rolled into the lava. The magma belched once then spit it back out. It landed near Old Scratch's feet and immediately began to complain. Old Gooseberry slowly looked up, the weapon falling from his nerveless fingers as another head sprouted up from the gash.

"That freakin' asshole just cut my head off!" shouted the head near his feet.

"No shit, man!" confirmed the head looming over the Devil.

Satan stared without hope at the thing that would not die.

He couldn't kill it nor could he escape it, either. The Prince of Darkness felt the cry grow in the darkness that once held his soul until it traveled up into his throat and out his mouth. The sound was an ear piercing shriek of defeat and only one thing could be heard above its' pathetic tone.

"What a freakin' candy ass, Bro. He screams like a girl..."

Satan awoke with a start, gulping in huge draughts of air while desperately trying to still his shaking body. Sweat pouring off him collected on his mahogany desk. He attempted to call Myco but his constricted throat barely let out the air from his lungs never mind the imp's name. No. He would not allow the Dean's access to his house and would do anything...*anything*... to keep them out. He reached into the side panel of his desk and took out a bottle of Scotch spilling it as he tried to get the opening to his mouth with his shaking hands. He took several long swallows praying the liquid would calm his frazzled nerves. It finally did and gave him the courage to look out his window to make sure his world was still the same. It was. For now.

Friday ~ Lunchtime

Harry and Rex caught up with a terrified Eli the next day. Eli not only gave Harry his money but also a number of broken teeth, a pint of blood and a handful of hair. Satisfied with their withdrawal, the brothers proceeded to their shared house where they dined on steaks and washed them down with the alcohol they had procured from the bar.

"That was some good eats," Rex stated, belching up dead cow and beer.

"Do you know the fool that jumped in front of my truck, Bro?"

"No…never saw him before in my life. You gave him a good shot, though," laughed Harry then winced for his face was still sore. His eye was beginning to open again.

"I think I busted his nose," stated Rex as he held his swollen knuckles up for both of them to see.

"Yeah -you sure did teach him a lesson or two!" Harry chortled, the whiskey slowly taking the edge off the pain.

The Prince of Darkness watched the pair reveling in his misery on one of his monitors, his dark mood becoming dourer with each passing second. He was oh so tempted to bring them here and spend eternity tormenting them for their transgressions. The lure grew stronger and only the unsettling dream stayed his decision. He began to smirk for he planned to visit them in the same guise that had landed him the broken nose and repay Rex for this particular violation. A thought suddenly erupted in his mind, one so troublesome that Satan felt a knot of trepidation grow in his stomach. There was a good chance that he would be unable to keep them out and his nightmare would come to fruition. His hands began to shake. He checked the time: 11 a.m. Thirty-one hours to go.

Friday ~ Midnight

Old Gooseberry narrowed his eyes at the figures darting in between the rows of houses. He watched as they comically stole from behind one shrub to the next lurching their way up Main Street toward the tenement house. The two shadows knew the area well; they had been born and raised in this section of town. The brick facades from a time gone by fronted a florist, restaurant, a video rental store and a nail salon. The tired building with the large grimy window was the Brick House, the neighborhood bar where the brothers have been hanging out since they were kids. When they were ten years old, they'd ask the drunks leaving the bar for change. The happy drunkard would stick his hand into his pocket and pull out a bunch of change. The brothers would slap at his hand sending the coins flying in all directions then proceed to pick up as many as they could before the inebriated man could focus long enough to grab at one of them.

That bar was where Rex first dabbled in the art of thievery, carrying off several bottles of beer, which the boys would drink in the bushes behind the park. Harry got so smashed one night that he tripped over his own feet and fell on top of a pile of beer bottles they had just shattered. The blood poured out of a shocked Harry's hand as a panicked Rex brought him home. Their father could smell the booze on them and knew what happened but had to wait to dispense any punishment until the doctor sewed up Harry's gash. Rex, in the meantime, convinced his father that they 'found' the beer and couldn't help themselves…drinking all the bottles before they realized what it was doing to them. Thinking boys will be boys, their father believed that the hangovers they would get the next day plus

Harry nearly bleeding to death would act as a deterrent. The only thing the boys learned was to throw the empties farther into the bushes.

The Prince of Darkness watched as the brothers left the Brick House swaying unsteadily in the early evening hours. Silent they were not.

"What do ya wanna do now, bro?"

"I gotta pee…"

"Hey! Watch it!" whispered Rex as Harry disappeared into the shadows of a building only to re-emerge and bump into his brother.

"How about now?"

"I wanna get laid."

"Well, Bro, you've pretty much…pretty…much… pissed off all of your girlfriends so you…you…you might have to double date yourself." Rex' belch was long, deep and reeked of beer and stale pretzels.

"I ain't gonna take care of my own business."

"We can go to Mary Cramer's house but…but…I get her first."

"You had her first the last time."

"Whatever. Let's go."

"We can cut through the Smith's backyard then hop over the fence behind the deli…it's fast and no one's gonna see us."

"Ain't they the ones with the grape vines?" asked Rex.

"Yeah…Auntie Jane still goes over there with leftovers so don't get any ideas," said Harry peering into the darkness, his blurred vision making the two door garage appear as if it had only one big door.

"She ain't gonna miss a few grapes, Bro."

They stumbled through Mrs. Smith's backyard; Rex spending a few moments picking several bunches of grapes and stashing them inside his shirt before they moved on. They used an old potting bench to get over the fence but Harry's pant leg became caught just as he was heaving himself over it. He tumbled into the deli's dumpster, the fence refusing to yield the hold on his trouser kept him hanging at an odd angle. He flailed his arms, seeking any sort of support but his hands found nothing but a ripped open garbage bag full of slimy cold cuts, a jar of rancid mayonnaise and a pile of soggy rolls.

"Rex! Hurry up, man, git me out of this thing!"

Harry's muted shouts spurred Rex into action and, although he managed to clear the fence, he misjudged the distance to the dumpster and crashed chest first into it. He didn't notice the thin shadow chuckling off to the side nor had he felt the slight push that re-directed his course when he jumped. Rex felt every grape rupture in his shirt upon impact. He cringed as the cold pulp spread across his chest. He shuddered as he placed his hand against his shirt and felt the seeds and skins. Rex reached up, quickly unhooked Harry then ripped open his shirt.

"This is so freakin' gross, Bro," he said flicking away the lumpy remnants from his skin. "I can't, man, I gotta go take a shower!"

"We're almost there!"

"Bullshit! This is nasty!"

"Shower at Mary's!"

Lucifer smirked for that little extra push he had given Rex

had been just enough to squash the grapes. His grin grew wider as he watched his favorite creations, maggots, cling to Harry's perspiration soaked shirt.

"But not as nasty as those freakin' things on your shoulders, Bro!" Rex' face twisted with nausea as he backed away from Harry who gave a choked, girlish scream. He tore off his shirt, maniacally brushing at the now gone insects he felt were still crawling all over him. Lucifer's features became dark and scheming for he knew exactly how he would penalize these two if they ended up in his house. The game was, for this night anyway, over.

"You freakin' wimp," muttered Rex as they walked down the street back toward the bar.

"*I'm* a wimp? You freakin' cried over squished grapes!"

"Afraid of a freakin' bug you asshole."

"Screw you," replied Harry then flinched in alarm as a moth flew by his head, the look of panic on his face sending the Devil into such a bout of laughter he thought his chest and sides would explode. For a split second, the Prince of Darkness actually wanted the pair in his house for an eternity of boundless amusement.

"Candy ass…"

"Freakin' asshole…" They rounded a corner and the night became quiet once more, silent except for what sounded like far-off laughter.

~

God and Michael walked through Heaven benevolently

greeting those who shared it with them. There was peace and calm here, the sounds of joyful laughter mingling well with the contented conversations between families and friends. They turned around as a newest family member entered the Gates, enthusiastically greeted by relatives who had long ago departed the land of the living.

"Goosie has been rather quiet, Boss," stated Michael as the two of them stopped and peered down from the clouds.

"Indeed he has, Michael. Anything I should know about?"

"He's doing rather well, considering the circumstances. It is not easy playing guardian angel to those two, Boss." Michael desperately tried to squelch a bout of laughter. The best he could do was to look away and cough into his clenched fist.

"I hear he has a few keepsakes from his endeavors...are you ill, Michael?" God asked when the Archangel abruptly dropped to his knees, his shoulders quivering.

"No, Boss..." Michael wiped the tears from his eyes, "I'm just offering Goosie," he sniffed then cleared his throat, "an extra prayer."

"How very kind of you."

Michael squeezed his eyes shut, hoping that God would change the subject before he lost complete control of himself.

"How long before this wager is over?"

"Another eighteen hours, Boss," replied Michael as he straightened up and rubbed his lower back. The flights back and forth to earth were taking their toll on him. He enjoyed flying but the sudden bursts of speed he needed to get from Heaven to the Deans were something he was not used to.

"I can have Gabriel take over for a while," suggested God.

"No, Boss, I wouldn't miss this for anything."

God lifted an eyebrow at the Archangel.

"What I meant was…"

"I know what you meant, Michael. I think that Lucifer has been creating a strategy to help him overcome his unavoidable future." He adjusted a fold in his robe while allowing himself a slight smile of satisfaction. Harry and Rex could not possibly be kept in check for an hour let alone three days, but he had to give Lucifer credit for trying. Besides, as long as he was preoccupied with the brothers he was less apt to wreak havoc elsewhere on earth. That result in itself might get Harry and Rex into Heaven but he was certainly not going to share that thought with anyone. He shuddered inwardly as he imagined the pair walking about Heaven with their halos askew, lifting up their robes to expose themselves to anyone who chanced by. They were proud of their family heirlooms and eager for others to see what He had given them.

"Boss?" asked Michael.

"I'm sorry, Michael…I was momentarily distracted."

"So I noticed, Boss. I just said that I was going to pay Goosie a visit…maybe discern a thing or two about his plans for Harry and Rex."

"Yes. That's a good idea, Michael." He watched the Archangel fly down to the land of the living then smiled as Joan of Arc approached Him.

"Michael has been quite busy of late, Lord," she stated in a soft voice that belied the courage thriving in her breast.

"Yes, child."

"Rumor has it that he has been spending time with the

Dark One, Lord," she continued.

"We have always kept an eye on Lucifer, Joan, you know that."

"Yes, Lord, but there have been…*rumors* of late."

"What kind of 'rumors'?"

"About the Deans." She whispered the words as if fearing they would hear her.

"What about them?" persisted God, keenly interested as to what talk was circulating amongst the clouds. The one thing that could not be checked at the Pearly Gates was Mankind's desire to gossip and the last thing he needed was for any hearsay to get around Heaven.

"Well," she began, "it is speculated that the reason Michael is spending so much time with the Dark One is because the Prince of Darkness is trying to force the Deans brothers up here."

"My child, what are the chances of that happening?"

"Miracles do happen, Lord."

"The blind can be made to see and those afflicted with leprosy can be cured, Joan. Those are miracles. Even Vegas would shy away from laying down odds that the Deans will end up here."

"Vegas has lost its proverbial shirt on more than one occasion by betting against such long odds, Lord."

"I understand, child, but you needn't worry."

She offered Him a respectful nod then walked away, God's eyes firmly fixed to the back of her head. She spoke for many, He knew, and the rumors would only grow as time passed until the Deans were firmly contained in Hell. Even then, there would be whispered chatter about how they 'almost' ended up here. Unlike Hell, there were no tunnels in which to seal them. God suddenly realized he had not breathed in several long moments.

Saturday ~ 6 hours to go

Harry roused himself from within the crumpled sheets and headed for the bathroom. He peered into Rex' tiny bedroom and grinned at the contorted shape under the covers. He scratched his groin and made his way to the kitchenette. He found a chipped blue mug in the mountain of dishes in the sink and rinsed it out while the pot filled with coffee.

"Hey! Bro! Get your ass up!"

"Yeah...what?"

"Here."

Rex took the proffered cup then shoved a pile of dirty clothes off the faded yellow and brown plaid couch. He sat down and sipped from his mug. It took several minutes to poke through the magazines and half-eaten bags of chips to locate the clicker. Rex looked up as something slid down the pile in the sink and crashed onto the floor in the kitchen. Harry joined him with his steaming cup of coffee in hand.

"What do you wanna do today?"

"Just hang out here for a while," replied Rex.

"You wanna go to Mackie's later?"

"Yeah."

The brothers left the apartment in the late morning, the Devil in furtive pursuit. Old Gooseberry followed them into the shabby restaurant beneath a washed out awning and took a seat at the counter. Lucifer rested his elbows on the top, recoiling as his skin touched brown sticky rings and blobs of yellow and red. He reached for the dispenser and ended up pulling the first few layers of soiled napkins out before reaching the clean ones. Old

Scratch scrubbed at the gunk permanently fused with the speckled countertop to no avail.

He tugged the brim of his baseball cap lower over his eyes and dropped his head until the hood of his sweatshirt swallowed half of his face and neck. Old Gooseberry could see the brothers sitting behind him by their reflection in the mirror behind the counter. The brothers ordered enough eggs, bacon, ham, hash and toast to feed a small country, washing all that food down with cup after cup of coffee. Lucifer rolled his eyes as the caffeine brought them to full wakefulness. *Well, at least you two are in here and out of trouble. With any luck, you'll be too full to do anything I'll regret.*

Harry and Rex mopped up the last of the egg yolk on their plates with toast corners then leaned back in satisfaction, their bulging stomachs straining against their tee shirts.

"Know what I could go for now, Bro?"

"A cigarette and a piece of ass?" replied Harry.

"Na-unh…a cigarette and a nap."

"You just got up!"

"Yeah…well."

"I think she wants me."

"Who?"

"The waitress. Watch."

The server walked past their table holding a freshly brewed pot of coffee in one hand, her ample butt brushing up against Harry's hand. She glared down at his smirking face then leaned seductively toward him.

"You do that again," she purred, her eyes sparking with

anger, "and I'll pour this on your crotch. Got it?" She turned and marched away before he could muster a response.

"I told you she wants me...I had to tell her 'no', though," laughed Harry as he and Rex walked out of the restaurant without paying the bill.

Old Scratch mumbled dark and disturbing things under his breath as he dropped twenty dollars onto the brothers' now vacant table and followed them out.

"Yo, Bro," Rex nudged Harry's arm, "why don't we hit the casino?"

"You got extra cash?"

Rex held up a fistful of twenties.

~

The brothers entered the Newport casino less than an hour later and headed upstairs to the smoking section. Colored lights flashed all around them and the myriad of sounds from the machines made it difficult to hear each other talk. They opted for a couple of machines near the bar.

"I'll buy this round."

"You better," replied Harry.

Harry glanced around the room then took the drink from Rex. Sticking a twenty-dollar bill into the slot, Harry took a sip from his glass then spun the wheels.

The Prince of Darkness watched them from behind a set of slot machines in the darkest section of the room. He tapped a finger to launch the spin on his machine.

"You're cheating the casino out of your money, Goosie."

"It's my vice."

"Yes, it is."

Michael and the Devil noticed Harry heading to the bar. He returned a few moments later with another round of drinks. The pair fed the machine twenty dollar bills with one hand and drank with the other.

"You might have to drive the boy's home, Goosie."

Old Gooseberry muttered something unintelligible under his breath.

"It would be a shame if they got into an accident so close to the end of the bet."

Old Scratch checked his watch: it was only four o' clock.

"A two for one special."

The Prince of Darkness massaged his temples.

"Do you smell smoke?"

Old Gooseberry instinctively patted the top of his head. He glared at the Archangel then peeked over at the brothers. Harry carried the empty glasses back to the bar, his gaze fixed on the Prince of Darkness.

"That's enough," hissed the Devil then intersected Harry near the bar.

Harry stared at him for several long seconds until recognition registered on his face. "You're the asshole from the other night!"

Old Scratch feigned panic as he slowly backed away from Harry.

"Yo! Bro! It's the freakin' idiot again!"

Rex walked over to his brother. "What the freak do you want? Why're you following us?"

"I'm not following you."

Michael watched a pair of security guards approach. Rex and Harry turned their attention from their foe to the guards, allowing Old Gooseberry a chance to sneak behind a row of machines.

"What seems to be the problem?" The older of the two sucked in his gut and pulled the waistband of his pants up and over it.

"Nothin'." Rex gazed around the room. "We're leaving."

The brothers stepped on the escalator, the mirrored passageway reflecting their disappointing faces.

"You go get the truck and I'll see if I can spot that little jerk," said Rex.

Harry headed for the door while Rex scanned the glassed-in lobby for the idiot following them. He noticed an elderly woman leaning on a walker a few feet away from him. Several teens crowded onto a couch next to her, their fingers speeding across their cell phone key pads.

"Lookit this shit," he muttered then walked over to the young adults. "Let the lady sit down."

One of the girls popped her gum; the boys gave him an indifferent expression.

"Get your asses off the couch and let her sit down!"

He glared at the slowly retreating teens, their surly remarks rewarded with a menacing scowl. Rex gently guided the woman to the sofa and helped her take her seat.

"Thank you."

"Your welcome."

"Will you join me for a moment?"

Rex glanced outside but Harry hadn't yet pulled up to the curb in front of the building. He sat down beside her.

"Today's my birthday."

"Happy birthday. How old are you?"

"I'm eighty-nine," she replied while adjusting her flowered scarf. "My daughter took me out for lunch in the restaurant upstairs."

Rex nodded.

"Do you believe in God, young man?" she asked after a long pause.

"What?"

"God. Do you believe in Him?"

"Uh…"

"He has blessed me with a wonderful life and a loving family."

"That's nice."

"Oh! There's my daughter. Thank you for indulging an old woman, young man, and may God bless you."

Rex helped her to her feet then nodded at the graying woman who escorted the birthday girl out. He cocked his head and pressed his lips together, her question reverberating in his mind. Harry pulled up and motioned to him. Rex entered the truck, remaining silent for several miles.

The Devil stepped behind one of the gigantic pillars supporting the roof over the carport and watched the brothers.

"Did you find that little asshole?"

"No."

"Screw him," stated Harry. "Let's get the freak outta here."

Old Gooseberry sighed as the pair left the parking lot, suddenly aware that Michael stood behind him.

"Did you see that, Mikey? Kindness. From Rex."

"I don't think that's enough to satisfy the agreement, Goosie."

"Maybe not, but there's hope for me yet!"

"Perhaps if they helped a few thousand more elderly ladies in the next two hours...."

"Don't pee on my parade, Mikey."

Michael smiled.

"We're done here." The Prince of Darkness abruptly disappeared.

~

The brothers headed for home, their enthusiasm dampened by the machines at the casino refusing to yield a quick buck and the reappearance of the weird guy.

"What's eatin' you, Bro?"

"Do you believe in God?" asked Rex.

"What kinda question is that?"

Rex told him about the old woman. "She ain't got no regrets, Bro."

Harry mulled over Rex' words. "I don't know...I guess a

little bit."

Harry pursed his lips; Rex flipped his lighter between his fingers. The broken lane markers on the highway blurred into a single yellow line. Harry turned on his right signal then merged onto the interstate heading east.

"Hey! Wanna go to Mackie's?" asked Rex lighting a cigarette.

"You buyin'?"

Saturday ~ 5:55 p.m.

Lucifer sat on a bench across the street from Mackie's, surrounded by a cannon, a boulder mounted with a plaque honoring the local soldiers and an American flag. A broad elm tree shaded him from the setting sun. He adjusted his dark blue baseball cap emblazoned with a red and white 'B', pulling the visor down lower as Harry's blue truck went by. The brothers turned down onto the side street adjacent to the bar and parked the vehicle. The Prince of Darkness checked his watch: 5:55.17. This will all be over in four minutes forty-three seconds.

Rex and Harry exited the truck, their boisterous laughter like nails on a chalkboard in Lucifer's ears. He'd go mad if forced to listen to that raucous noise for eternity. Hell, he would even consider banging on the Pearly Gates until his hands bled, begging to be admitted to that fluffy place rather than spend one minute with them. A movement on the sidewalk to the left of the bar caught Old Gooseberry's interest. A little girl, perhaps three years old, rode her yellow tricycle with multi-colored streamers toward the bar. A purple barrette held her blonde curls off her face but the hair along the sides and back floated freely as she pedaled along. She wore a pair of pink shorts, a flowered tank top and a grape Popsicle mustache.

"Pay attention...don't get sidetracked...one good deed... you can do this."

Rex and Harry turned the corner. Rex planted his right foot on the stoop, his right hand reaching for the handle. He suddenly backed away as a large group of patrons left the tavern. Clad in jeans and matching black tee shirts emblazoned with '2010 Champions' in white letters, the men and women continued to exit the bar. The brothers exchanged annoyed glances.

The little girl hummed to herself as she traveled on. The nearer she came to the bar the more her way became blocked. She steered her tricycle closer to the curb.

The crowd in front of the tavern spread out along the sidewalk, laughing and joking with each other as they waited for the remainder of their friends to join them. Harry and Rex gave up trying to enter the bar, lighting up cigarettes and talking to one another in front of the building instead. The Prince of Darkness looked at the time: 5:57.48. Two minutes twelve seconds left.

The little girl stopped several yards away from the group and looked up at the towering wall of denim and cotton, her lower lip swallowing the upper one. Old Gooseberry stared at her, inwardly urging her to get lost. She glanced over at Lucifer now sitting at the edge of the bench. She brushed a stray hair from across her forehead then waved at him. He looked into her eyes, the innocence radiating from within those sparkling sapphires captivating him. She smiled at him and he found himself returning the gesture.

"Hey! Wait your turn, assholes!"

The words broke the hold the little girl had on Lucifer, his mind returning to the task at hand. The Dean brothers, tired of waiting for the exodus to end tried to push their way through the throng. Pushing and shoving ensued followed by swearing and shouting. A fully loaded red and black gravel truck rolling up the road added its din to the growing chaos in front of Mackie's, the driver blaring the horn at a group of kids on bikes standing on the street corner. Time: 5:59.01.

The little girl glimpsed the adults blocking the sidewalk then turned her handlebars toward Lucifer. She headed out into the street beaming as she closed the distance between herself and the Prince of Darkness. The truck loomed over the child; the sound of gears grinding as the driver hastily downshifted harsh in the late afternoon air.

"Oh…shit…no kid…go back!" Lucifer shouted at her. His expression dropped as the little girl inexplicably stopped in the middle of the street.

Woe unto you if even just one innocent perishes…

The Prince of Darkness looked upon her face, the child's purity a luminous glow warming even the dark recess where his soul had, eons ago, resided. He lunged for the little girl.

Rex and Harry become aware of the child when the high-pitched squealing of tires ripped through the area. As one, they launched themselves toward the little girl, vaguely aware of another body hurtling at them from the opposite direction. They slid across the road, the uneven tar abrading their skin to the bone. Chrome and black and red paint filled their vision; the heat from the engine seared their flesh. The incessant blaring of a horn blocked out the screaming from the sidewalk. Then there was complete silence.

The time: 6:00.00 p.m.

~

Bouquets of flowers and dozens of candles lay strewn in front of Mackie's bar on either side of the stoop. Passersby glanced solemnly at the tire marks in the street. Whispers, both from actual eyewitnesses and unfounded suppositions hung in the hot summer air.

"There was so much blood."

"They didn't have a chance."

"I heard the tires squealing from my living room."

"I heard they're still picking body parts from the front of the truck."

"They were drunk."

"They were heroes."

The media interviewed whoever would offer a word then left to pursue the next catastrophe. After a few days, the flowers dried up and the candles burned out.

Saturday ~ 6:00.01 p.m.

A host of angels finished singing the hymn, their wondrous voices bringing a tear even to God's eyes. He sat on a throne of clouds and light, his benevolent gaze resting on all those gathered. Michael, clad in a snow-white gown stood across from him, his massive wings spread out. God peered at the newest arrival standing in front of the Archangel and smiled.

"Your unselfish act has granted you access to the Pearly Gates," the Lord spoke in kind tones. "Welcome, my son."

Michael folded his wings revealing a scrawny man dressed in a white robe, which hung limply from his gaunt frame. Bruises and scrapes covered the initiates' face. The Archangel crossed his arms over his muscular chest and grinned broadly.

"This isn't funny, G." The Devil scowled at the smirking angels.

"I disagree, Lucifer."

"C'mon, Goosie," Michael slapped him playfully on his back, "Lighten up! You'll be back home the second the proper paperwork has been filled out."

"'Paperwork'? Since when do you need forms to get my ass back down where I belong?" He shot the snickering angels a dark look.

"We have a system that must be strictly adhered to up here, Lucifer. No exceptions allowed."

"What of the Dean brothers?" asked the Prince of Darkness in tentative tones.

"Ah! The Dean brothers."

"Well?" demanded the Devil.

"Rex and Harry Dean survived, Lucifer, thanks to you."

"I knew it must have taken more than saving that little girl to get me up here. *And?*"

"They'll spend a few weeks first in the hospital then in rehab so you should be able to get some rest for a while."

"Terrific."

"Don't look so glum, Lucifer, it could have been much worse."

"Yeah, Goosie, you could be up here watching the Dean brothers sitting at your desk smoking your cigars and drinking your hootch!"

A shiver ran up Lucifer's spine. "Don't remind me."

The Prince of Darkness took a deep breath and looked around, wondering how half of those present managed to obtain a halo and a pair of wings. *How difficult would it be to recruit a few of these souls? Most of them just barely eked in anyway.* A slow smile crept onto his face while his fingers drew little circles along his sides. Joan took a step backward, her hand covering her mouth.

"Goosie?"

"Yes, Mikey?"

"Your powers don't work up here."

Old Gooseberry blinked several times, exhaled then dropped his head until his chin hit his chest. The flames on top of his head flashed, fizzled then went out.

Cheeky bastard!

The End